For lovely Lois – J.J.
For Dad x – L.C.

First published in Great Britain in 2014 by
Piccadilly Press, a Templar/Bonnier publishing company
Deepdene Lodge, Deepdene Avenue, Dorking, Surrey RH5 4AT
www.piccadillypress.co.uk

Text © Julia Jarman, 2014
Illustrations copyright © Lynne Chapman, 2014

Designed by janie louise hunt
Printed and bound in China by WKT
Colour reproduction by Dot Gradations

ISBN: 978 1 84812 403 5 (hardback)
ISBN: 978 1 84812 404 2 (paperback)

1 3 5 7 9 10 8 6 4 2

Jungle Grumble

JULIA JARMAN
LYNNE CHAPMAN

Piccadilly

Lion, King of the Jungle, was snoozing. But a noise disturbed his dream. It came from the waterhole.

Mutter!
Mutter!
Moan! Moan!

Snap! Snap!

Screech! Screech!

Groan!

All the animals were grumbling.
Lion couldn't get back to sleep,
so he went to see what all the
fuss was about.

"My nose is too long,"
moaned Aardvark.

"My bottom's too big," said Hippo. "And my tail is tiny. Feathers would be lovely."

Even Elephant, usually so sensible,
said she hated her wrinkly trunk.
"And grey's so dull."

"I'd like a change too," grumbled Zebra.
"I'm fed up with stripes."

Giraffe joined in *very*
glumly. "I'm much too tall.
It's my neck and my legs.
I wish they were shorter."

"You look fine just the way you are," said Lion.
But it didn't do any good. They went on grumbling till
he could stand it no longer.

"Enough!"
he roared.

"You all want to look different? Well, maybe I can help." For Lion had an idea.

A little while later, he called to the animals, "Come and look at this."

"It's a Swap Shop. You can swap
all the bits you don't like," said Lion.
"That's so fun!" said Parrot.
"It's got changing rooms and mirrors and …"
But the other animals were rushing in to see for themselves.

"Who wants my tiny tail?" cried Hippo.

"I want a long swishy one!"

"Who'd like my bottom?"
said Blue-Bottomed Monkey. "I'm so bored with blue.
I'd love pink wings like yours, Flamingo."

Lion wondered when they would be ready.
There seemed to be a lot of swapping going on.
Suddenly he roared, "Let's see what you look like!"

One by one, the animals
stepped out proudly.

SWAP SHOP

They adored
showing off
their new gear . . .

till the sun went down.

And then some of the animals started grumbling.

WHINGE!

WHINGE!

WHINGE!

"Croc keeps snapping
at my lovely long swishy
tail," said Hippo.

Moan!

Moan!

Moan!

"I'm hungry, but I can't
reach my favourite leaves,"
said Giraffe.

Whimper!
Whimper!

Blue-Bottomed Monkey suddenly
cried, "I need my bottom back!
Or I can't do a p—"
It wasn't long before *all* the animals
were whinging and moaning.

HOWL!

"Qui-et!" roared Lion.

"The Swap Shop's still there, if you want to change back."

WHOOSH! There was a stampede as all the animals rushed in.

Soon the animals were their normal selves again.

Later that night, they gathered
round the waterhole.
"My bottom's not so bad,"
Blue-Bottomed Monkey said.
"It's quite cool, really."

"So's my nose,"
said Aardvark.

"And I really like
my trunk," said Elephant.

"Great," sighed Lion.
"At last they're all happy.
I can't think why they wanted to look different."
And with that Lion yawned,
closed his eyes and began to dream . . .